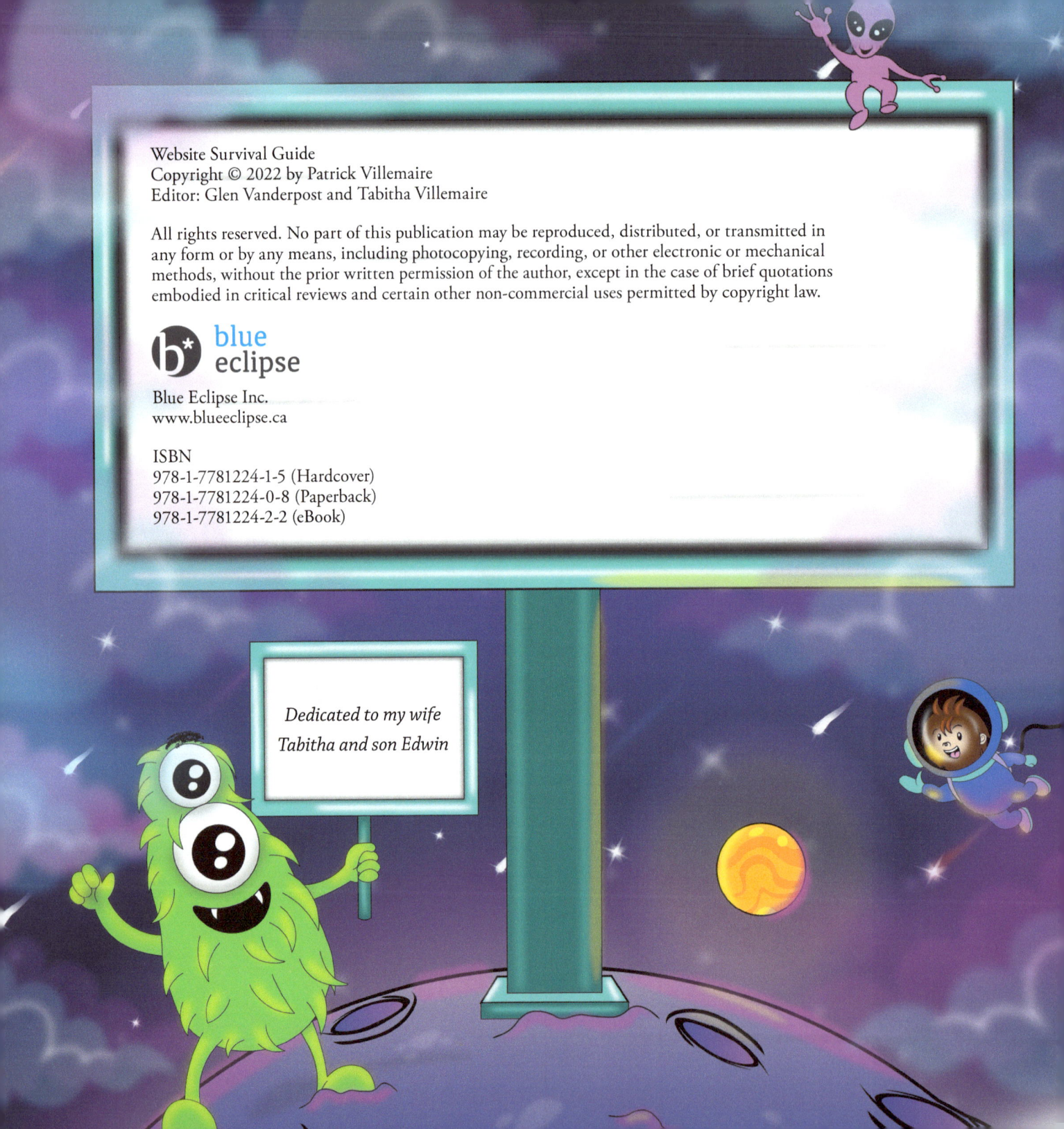

Website Survival Guide
Copyright © 2022 by Patrick Villemaire
Editor: Glen Vanderpost and Tabitha Villemaire

All rights reserved. No part of this publication may be reproduced, distributed, or transmitted in any form or by any means, including photocopying, recording, or other electronic or mechanical methods, without the prior written permission of the author, except in the case of brief quotations embodied in critical reviews and certain other non-commercial uses permitted by copyright law.

blue eclipse

Blue Eclipse Inc.
www.blueeclipse.ca

ISBN
978-1-7781224-1-5 (Hardcover)
978-1-7781224-0-8 (Paperback)
978-1-7781224-2-2 (eBook)

*Dedicated to my wife Tabitha and son Edwin*

# WEBSITE SURVIVAL GUIDE

## Steve's Magical Adventure

**WRITTEN BY -** PATRICK VILLEMAIRE

**EDITED BY -** GLEN VANDERPOST // TABITHA VILLEMAIRE

Meet intern Steve. Steve works at the biggest conglomerate you've ever seen! He is in charge of the marketing team.

"Build better websites for the thousands of businesses that we manage", they said. The words didn't motivate Steve, they filled him with dread!

From doctors and dentists to non-profit organizations; auto shops, retailers, and those who worked in space stations. Running websites for businesses large and small; he was now in charge of running them all.

Before the job started they gave him a list. "We want all of these things done and not a single one missed".

Steve was concerned the list would get to his head. "What about form and function", he said? And content and structure, there was none to be seen. "Don't worry about content", they said with glee, "we recycle all of that from a dusty old machine".

No goals, no targets, no optimization.

It was a recipe for disaster and that's no exaggeration!

They wanted *their* plan and what could he say? He didn't want to mess up on his very first day!

So Steve went into the forest, only meaning to take a quick break. He sat there for only a moment; he was sure he was still awake. He just wanted to clear his head to figure out his plan. He *knew* if he could get the job done that he would be the man!

That's when things all started to change. He came out of the bush a man rearranged.

A vision came to him of what he had to do. I'll make a website survival guide to help me get through! I'll fix all the sites and make them all work. I'll start from the top until they convert.

To management he went, to share the good news. Our journey starts now, so strap on your best shoes.

We'll have automated tools to collect all those 5-star reviews. Via email and text, we'll ask people to choose: ask them simple questions, get feedback and their news.

Catching negative reviews to make them all right, while responding to everyone, we appreciate their insight. Place reviews on your site to increase your authority and show off your might!

Then all at once, with no prior indication, the bosses all learned how to manage their reputation.

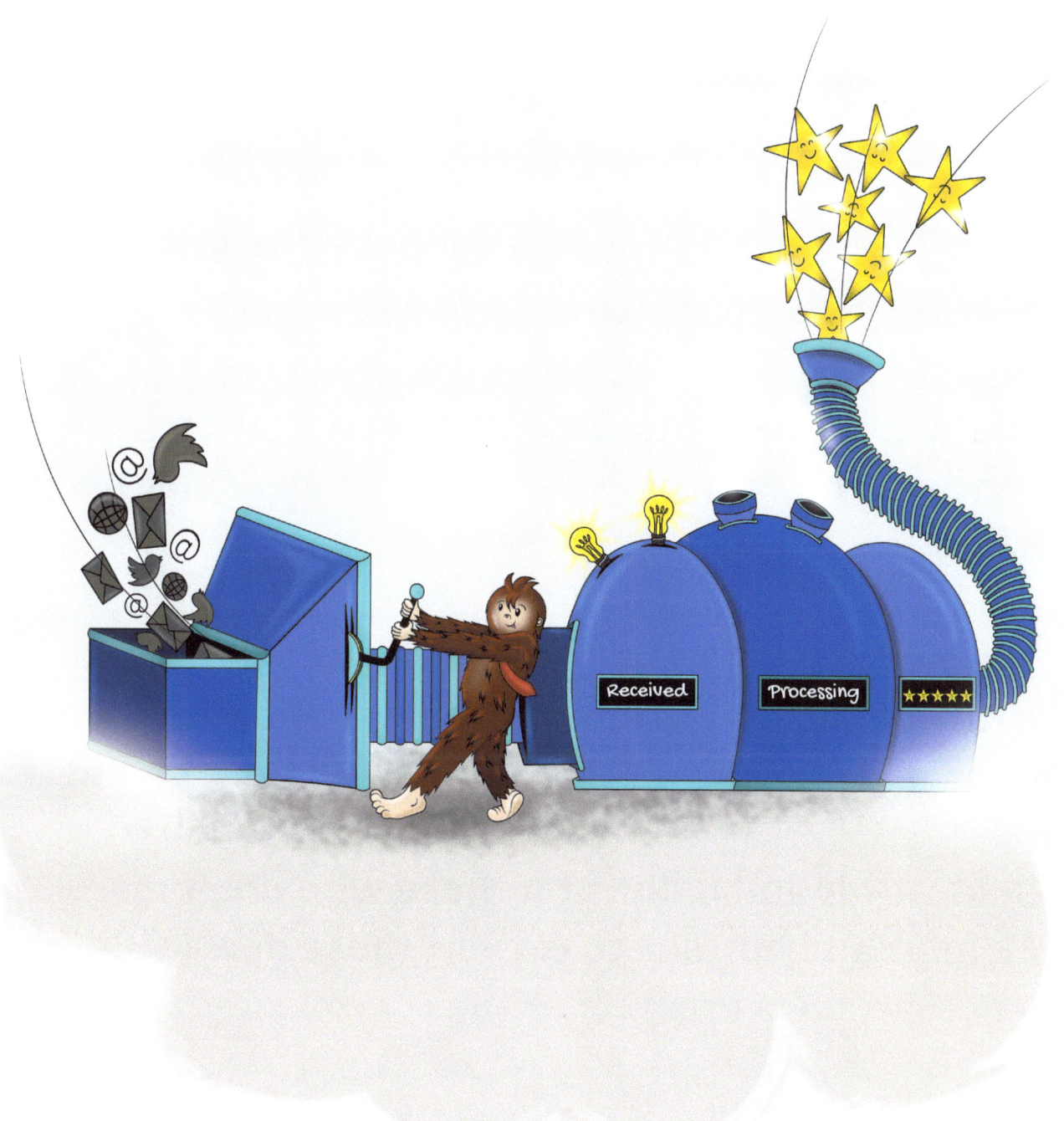

Content is King. It can make your heart sing. Without it, there is no point, we truly have no zing.

The message should be clear; keep it short and concise. The bosses were attentive and took his advice.

The next step to lead your customer down the path is to use keywords in headings and make an impact!

Bold words and bullets for those who don't read. Pictures and buttons to convert those new leads.

Search Engine Optimization is something we frequently use, it helps people find your site so they can easily peruse.

To get good reviews and have people link to you, use headings and bold terms to get your way through.

Write in plain language, in words your customers trust. Keep your website fresh and don't let it rust.

Localize your content and target your demographic. Run tools to scan for improvements, track data to understand your web traffic.

Smart and effective design has always been key, so make proper use of white space and imagery.

Smiling faces make us happy and are never a cliché. But avoid dull stock photos that are all made the same way.

When it comes to design, be playful and have fun. But most of all, support the content to get the job done.

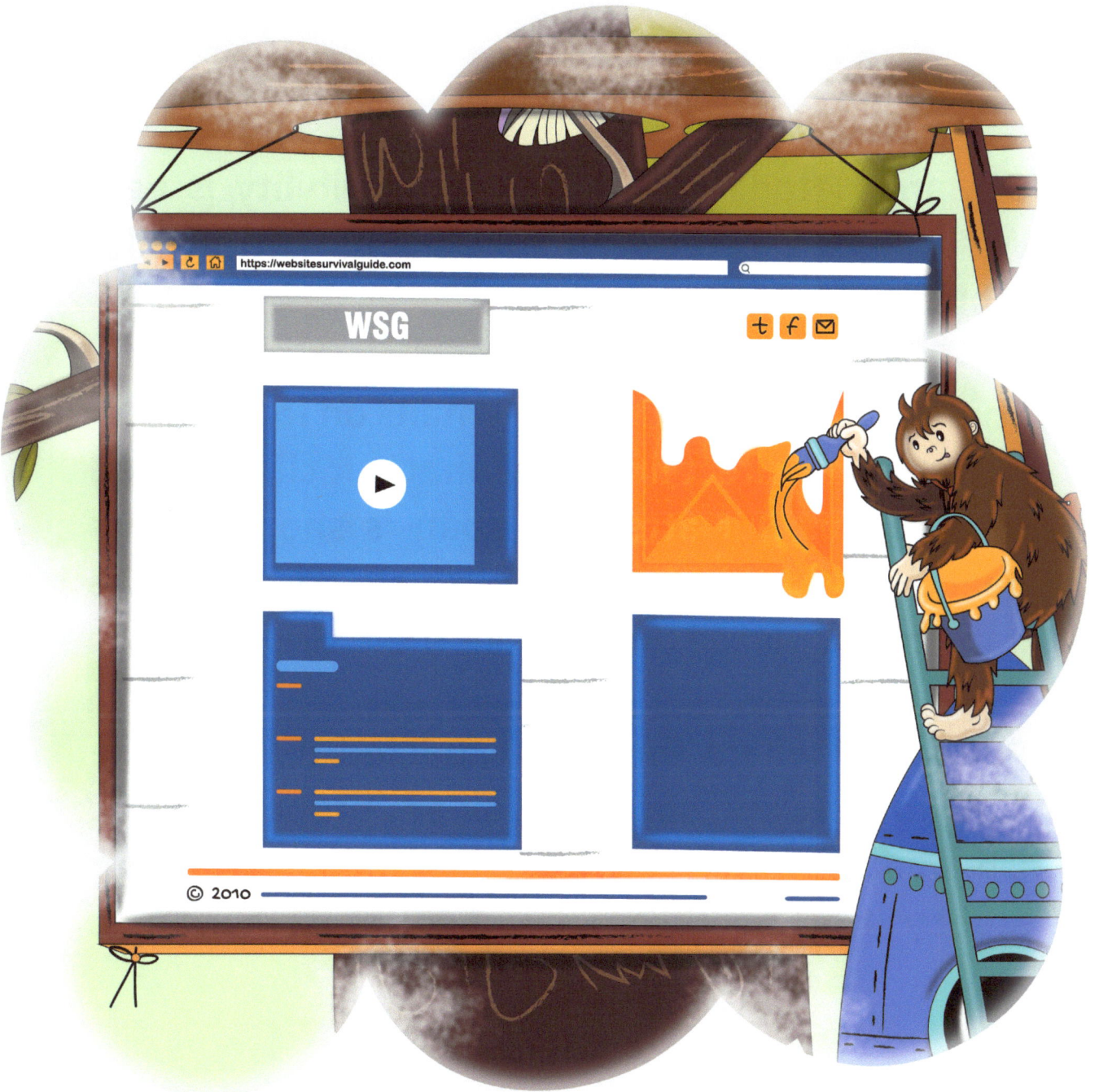

Oh, and details do matter, compatibility is key! We'll have a great web experience, on mobile, tablet and PC.

Confirmation messages and emails on forms; clear buttons and direct links are what our clients need to perform. Our attention span is short, clients need information in a wink. Customers are like baby birds, please don't make them think.

Put things where they are expected to be. Make sure spacing and sizing are all set proportionally. On smaller devices layouts can change, with our stubby little fingers sometimes you must rearrange.

People love filling in forms, said no one ever. A form is a form, it's always an endeavour.

Make them functional and capture just what you need. Ask thoughtful questions, and satisfaction will be guaranteed!

Converting paper to digital will help everyone. Format it for any device so they can fill it out on the run. A save and continue button might be nice; for those longer ones don't make them do it twice.

But most of all make it clear if there has been an error. "We can't submit", they screamed in terror. When it is all submitted correctly, congratulate them on a job well done. Filling forms is not so bad; it can be fun.

AB Split testing and analytics will be our conversion super tool. Testing different variations of elements to see which one will truly rule.

A gold or red button, the difference may be surprising. What if we try a different photo or change some text without compromising. If we test the right things we can increase our sales. Optimizing our site will make sure we don't fail.

There's so much to do. The jobs are so big. But a no-mess approach will help us get it done in a jig.

Some simple, small changes might be all that we need. With testing and optimization, we will convert all the new leads.

I have a grand plan, a checklist on paper, to build this little idea bigger than a skyscraper!

And when Steve was done, he heard the applause.
He had found his purpose, he knew his cause!

Helping businesses go from survive to thrive with his brand-new website survival guide!

**Before You Begin**

*Your web designer/agency can help you get everything ready before your site build, but to save time and money here is a list of things you can do:*

- ☐ Create a mood board
- ☐ Document branding/colour requirements
- ☐ Draft SEO keywords
- ☐ Final content is ready (or very close to ready)
    - ☐ OR use existing content
- ☐ Have a draft value proposition
- ☐ Have goals for your website and the desired actions to be taken by visitors
- ☐ Identify languages the website will be built in (i.e.: EN, FR, ES, etc)
- ☐ Identify target audience/market
- ☐ Images/icons are ready/purchased
- ☐ Provide logos
- ☐ Provide inspirational websites
- ☐ Provide a draft sitemap/list of pages required
- ☐ Identify if stock photos are required

**A/B Split Testing**

- ☐ Analytics tracking
- ☐ Criteria for choosing winning test
- ☐ List of test cases

**Accessibility Requirements**

- ☐ Follows WCAG AA
- ☐ Images have proper descriptions and alt text
- ☐ The design has proper contrast between text and background elements

**Business Planning**
- ☐ Create mission statement
- ☐ Create vision/targets
- ☐ Identify corporate values
- ☐ Marketing strategy/client acquisition
- ☐ Our process
- ☐ Services we offer
- ☐ Services we do not offer
- ☐ Target market/audience

**Design**
- ☐ Create style guide
    - ☐ Primary colours
    - ☐ Secondary colours
    - ☐ Accent colours / Call-to-action
    - ☐ Banner style & dimensions (homepage / subpage)
    - ☐ Primary font
    - ☐ Secondary font
- ☐ Confirmation messages (most people forget these!)
- ☐ Imagery selected
- ☐ Icons selected
- ☐ Mobile/tablet design
- ☐ Wireframes
- ☐ 404 page

**Implementing Features** - unique per project
- ☐ Advanced search and filter functions
- ☐ Accessibility tool
- ☐ Analytics / heat mapping (ie: Google Analytics, Hotjar, etc)
- ☐ Blog
- ☐ Commenting ability

- ☐ Current news section
- ☐ Ecommerce support
- ☐ Events calendar
- ☐ Favourites section
- ☐ Forms (i.e.: contact)
- ☐ Glossary function
- ☐ Login/register functionality
- ☐ Member's portal
- ☐ Newsfeed
- ☐ Resources library
- ☐ Reviews/testimonials
- ☐ Sharing on social media
- ☐ Site search
- ☐ Social media feeds
- ☐ SSO setup (single sign-on)
- ☐ Submission of posts by members
- ☐ Other

## Mobile Checklist
- ☐ Content stacked on mobile (list any exceptions)
- ☐ Key elements to include in the header (logo, phone, menu icon)
- ☐ Menu position (slide from the left side, slide down, etc)
- ☐ Phone numbers are clickable links
- ☐ Site tested on mobile/tablet
- ☐ Take screenshots of different screen sizes
- ☐ Other considerations

## Ongoing Support & Maintenance
- ☐ Additional IT services (ie: Email support)
- ☐ Analytics review
- ☐ Daily website backups

- ☐ Monthly security updates (at a minimum)
- ☐ Ongoing website support package
- ☐ Strategic consultations
- ☐ Training sessions
- ☐ Web hosting

**Reputation Management**
- ☐ Display reviews on your website
- ☐ Have a Google My Business account
- ☐ Identify networks to collect reviews on (ie: Google, Facebook)
- ☐ Respond to all reviews
- ☐ Strategy for collecting reviews
- ☐ Strategy for intercepting negative reviews

**SEO / Content Checklist**
- ☐ Clear value proposition
- ☐ Clear call-to-actions
- ☐ Content uses plain language
- ☐ Content is skimmable (proper use of headings, bolding, bullets, etc)
- ☐ List of keywords
- ☐ Mission statement
- ☐ Proper HTML structure (Heading 1 > Heading 2 > Heading 3, etc)
- ☐ Site name in the browser bar
- ☐ Site tagline
- ☐ Target ideal customers/industries
- ☐ Use of bolding for keywords

## About the Author

Patrick Villemaire is the creator of the Website Survival Guide and the founder of Blue Eclipse Inc, a web agency based in Ottawa, Canada. His passion is making the web a better place and he has been building websites for over 20 years.

Patrick is a graduate of McMaster University with a double major in Multimedia and Communications, and a minor in English. When not building websites he is busy enjoying life with his wife, son and barking dog.

---

## How we can help you

A traditional web design agency based in Canada. We strive to make websites that are easy-to-use, and converts visitors to highly qualified leads.

Don't settle on building your website. We provide template parts for you to choose from so you can mix and match to build your website!

We don't build websites, we transform businesses! Training and consulting services to take your online presence from survive to thrive.

**blueeclipse.ca**

**websitefuel.ca**

**websitesurvivalguide.com**

www.ingramcontent.com/pod-product-compliance
Lightning Source LLC
LaVergne TN
LVHW071651060526
838200LV00029B/426